Magic Pony

Patients on Wheels

"Watch out!" shouted Nasty Granger, and Pete swung easily away, still waving, following Spike with stylish lazy footwork. "It's your bag." They've taken your bag." The lady clearly didn't understand what she was shouting about. This left Katy no choice. She didn't wait for the boys to be discovered. She raced after the rollerblades as fast as she could

Magic Pony

Thieves on Wheels

"Watch out!" shouted Natty. Granger and Pete swung easily away, still waving, following Spike with stylish, lazy footwork. "It's your bag! They've taken your bag!" The lady clearly didn't understand what she was shouting about. This left Natty no choice. She didn't wait for the loss to be discovered. She raced after the rollerbladers as fast as she could.

Follow all of Natty and Ned's adventures!
Collect all the fantastic books in the
Magic Pony series:

Magic Pony

Thieves on Wheels

ELIZABETH LINDSAY

Illustrated by Peter Kavanagh

■SCHOLASTIC

For William

Scholastic Children's Books,
Euston House, 24 Eversholt Street,
London NW1 1DB, UK
A division of Scholastic Ltd
London ~ New York ~ Toronto ~ Sydney ~ Auckland
Mexico City ~ New Delhi ~ Hong Kong

First published in the UK by Scholastic Ltd, 1999
This edition published in the UK by Scholastic Ltd, 2005

Text copyright © Elizabeth Lindsay, 1999
Illustrations copyright © Peter Kavanagh, 1999

10 digit ISBN 0 439 95980 2
13 digit ISBN 978 0439 95980 3
Fairs edition 10 digit ISBN 0 439 95102 X
Fairs edition 13 digit ISBN 978 439 95102 9

Printed and bound by Nørhaven Paperback A/S, Denmark

2 4 6 8 10 9 7 5 3 1

Contents

Chapter 1

Rollerbladers

By the time the bus turned into the
bus station, Natty was coming to
the end of an exciting pretend.
She had been galloping across the
countryside, jumping wide hedges
and leaping deep ditches, on her
magic pony Ned. She wished it
would happen in real life but Ned

had remained in his pony poster on her bedroom wall for a whole week, with not a glimmer of the magic that would turn him into the real live pony she loved so much. Natty hoped his magic hadn't run out and that he wouldn't stay a pony in a picture for ever. Pretends were fun but real magic was best.

The bus stopped and Jamie gave her a dig. "Come on, dreamer, we're here."

"I can see," Natty said, looking out of the window and standing up.

Mum led the way. "Best foot forward, you two."

She was taking them shopping in town to buy new trainers because both Natty and Jamie's feet had grown bigger. Jamie, whose feet were the largest, had laughed when Natty suggested that one day her feet might catch his up.

"Never, because I'm older and bigger and a boy!"

Natty had wriggled her toes, deciding to wait and see. Most of the time she liked having an older brother, especially one who was a conjurer and was going to be a famous magician when he grew up. It made him special, and even Penelope Potter, whose pony Pebbles lived in the field opposite Natty's house, thought so too.

Natty sighed, feeling suddenly sorry for herself. It was all right for Penelope. She could ride her dapple grey pony whenever she liked. Penelope didn't have to wait for magic to happen. Natty shuffled behind Jamie towards the front of the bus. On the other hand, Pebbles couldn't talk and he couldn't go from big to small like Ned. And it wasn't only Ned who went from big to small. If Natty was riding him and he magicked himself tiny, Ned magicked her tiny too, which was extraordinary.

Having reminded herself of all the wonderful things Ned's magic could do, Natty no longer felt sorry for herself. What did it matter if she had to wait? The waiting was worth it, and she jumped from the bus with a big grin on her face.

"We'll try out the new Shopping Mall," said Mum. "I read in the paper it's got three shoe shops. We're bound to find you trainers there."

Natty would have preferred to look in Old Market Square, with its rambling stalls and interesting alleyways. Jamie, too, was looking longingly along the road that would take them there. Natty knew he wanted to go to Cosby's Magic

Emporium and try out magic tricks in Mr Cosby's shop, a far more interesting thing to do than buying new trainers. Natty would have liked to have visited Mr Cosby as well, to tell him how pleased she was with her special pony poster. As pleased as Mr Cosby had said she would be on the day she had bought it from him.

Ned had sworn her to secrecy about his special magic and so, naturally, she had told no one. She took special care of the poster, keeping it pinned safely above her chest of drawers, and in return

Ned took special care of her and had taught her to ride.

"You're dawdling, Natty," called Mum. "I don't want you getting lost in the Mall."

Natty skipped to catch up, and as she did so she was overtaken by three big boys whirling past on rollerblades. They came so close that they almost spun her off balance and she was left to stare after them while her ears hummed with the drone of wheels on tarmac.

"Natty!" Jamie shouted. The boy at the back glanced over his shoulder and Natty was startled by

his black spiky hair and leering grin.
She hurried to catch up.

"Did you see the rollerbladers?"
she asked.

Jamie grinned. "Dead cool."

"They nearly knocked me over!"

"Then stay close," said Mum, "in case they come back."

Natty felt safer once they were inside the Shopping Mall, waiting while Mum looked up shoe shops on the map.

"Would you buy rollerblades?" she asked, knowing how good Jamie was at saving up.

"I would if I didn't want a Magic Vanishing Box more," he said. "It's a great trick but costs loads."

"Now, keep up," said Mum, setting off along the shiny wide walkway between the shops. "We're going up to the next floor. We'll buy the trainers first, then Jamie can go to Mr Cosby's. After that, if there's time before the bus, we'll have jam doughnuts at the Steamy Café."

"Jam doughnuts!" Natty cried, skipping beside Mum, who was steering them towards a gleaming silver escalator. "Can I have Coke as well?"

"We'll see," Mum hedged.

Beside the escalator a fountain sprayed tall jets of green water higher than the top of the balcony. The water, Natty realized, was slowly changing to blue.

"How does it do that?" she gasped.

"No idea," said Jamie, as impressed as she was.

There were lots of shoppers strolling about and Mum ended up on the escalator before they did. There was a whirr of rollerblade wheels and Natty jumped to the safety of the moving stairs before turning to watch the same three boys loop and twirl around the shoppers on the ground floor.

"They'd better watch out," said Jamie, jumping on behind her. "There was a sign on the way in that said 'No Rollerblading.'"

The boys were slick and impressive, and two of them wore helmets and elbow pads. The boy with the black spiky hair had the words MAN OF SPEED blazoned in red and gold letters across the front of his grubby white T-shirt. Mesmerized, Natty gazed after him as he whizzed by the bottom of the escalator. She was so engrossed, she almost missed the moment to jump off.

She and Jamie caught up with Mum and all three of them looked down over the balcony. The boys

were circling close to an old lady,
swinging their arms in a kind of
weaving dance, until one of
them tripped and knocked into her.
At once the boy with the spiky hair
took the old lady's elbow and, with
an easy grace, steadied her.

The old lady shook him off. "You young hooligans!" she cried with a voice so loud, they heard it above the splashing of the fountain. "You nearly knocked me over!"

"Oh, help!" cried Natty. "It's Mrs Plumley!" And before either Mum or Jamie could stop her, she set off at a run, racing round the balcony to the Down escalator.

Chapter 2

The Empty Bag

Natty squeezed between the shoppers on the moving stairs, racing on down when she had the chance. At the bottom she turned this way and that but Mrs Plumley was gone. Then she saw Jamie leaning over the balcony and pointing. Running in the direction he indicated she was in time to see the familiar figure of her friend from next door swallowed by the crowd.

"Mrs Plumley," she called. "Wait!"

On hearing her name, Mrs Plumley turned back, her face lighting up when she saw who it was. "Natty, dear! How nice to see you."

"Are you all right? I saw the rollerbladers."

"The cheeky young scamps. They almost had me over, but, yes, I'm fine, thank you, my love."

"Where's Ruddles?" Natty asked, curious because usually Mrs

Plumley took her little dog everywhere with her.

"No dogs allowed in the Shopping Mall, Natty. Ruddles is tucked up at home, safe in his basket. You're not here on your own, are you?"

"No, I'm with Mum and Jamie. We've come to buy trainers."

"Oh, and there they are!" said Mrs Plumley with a smile as she returned a wave from Mum and Jamie, who were on the Down escalator.

"What have you come to buy?" Natty asked.

"A birthday present for my granddaughter Lucy. She's told me what she wants. It's a pony book. You may have heard of it. I've got the title written down on a piece of paper." Mrs Plumley opened her shopping bag and rummaged inside. "I put it in my purse. It's in here somewhere." She held a handle in each hand and began to look anxiously into the bag. "Well, it was in here. Can you see it, Natty?"

Natty looked inside. Apart from a plastic carrier, the shopping bag was empty.

"There's no purse in here," said Natty. "Have you put it in your pocket?"

Mrs Plumley patted her coat to make sure. "No, I always carry it in my shopping bag. I had it when I went to the Post Office because I put my pension money in it."

"Is everything all right?" Mum asked, arriving full of concern. "Those boys ought to be reported."

"Nuisances on wheels, aren't they?" said Mrs Plumley, more concerned with looking in her bag. "I seem to have done a silly thing."

"Mrs Plumley's lost her purse," said Natty. "It's full of pension money." She gave Jamie a nudge and, while Mum helped Mrs Plumley look in her shopping bag one more time, they started a search of the floor, glancing between the legs of the passing shoppers, hoping to see the missing purse. They went as far as the fountain but with no luck.

"If it fell out of her bag it could be anywhere," said Jamie. "What does it look like?"

"It's brown and square and quite big," said Natty, remembering the purse from the times she had seen it on Mrs Plumley's living-room table. "Maybe she left it on the counter in the Post Office?"

"Or maybe it's been stolen!"

"Stolen?" gasped Natty. "But who would steal it?"

"The rollerbladers," said Jamie. "They were close enough to put their hands in her bag."

"But they wouldn't have, would they?"

Jamie shrugged. "Well, the purse has gone. It would have been easy to do. That boy with the spiky hair got really close."

"But he was helping Mrs Plumley after the other boy knocked into her."

"Exactly," said Jamie. "If you distract a person by knocking into them and then pretend to help them—"

"Like the boy with the spiky hair did!"

"Just like… It's a perfect moment to put your hand in their bag."

"But that's terrible!" said Natty, her eyes widening. "I just hope they didn't, that's all."

They went back to find Mum with her arm round Mrs Plumley's shoulder.

"We're taking Mrs Plumley to the police station in case someone hands in the purse," said Mum.

"I feel all of aflutter," said Mrs Plumley. "Everything gone – pension book, bus pass, all my money. And what about Lucy's birthday present? What was that book called? 'Dear Pony' or was it 'Cream Pony'? I can't remember!"

"*Dream Pony*," said Natty. "I've read that one. It's brilliant."

"Oh, Natty, I do believe it was.

But now all my money's gone, I can't buy it! And Lucy's coming for her birthday tea tomorrow!"

Mum linked arms with Mrs Plumley. "Don't you worry about a thing. I can lend you some money.

But first, let's report your lost purse. You never know, someone may have handed it in already."

Natty and Jamie exchanged glances. They were wondering if that was likely but they obediently followed on behind Mum and Mrs Plumley as they made their way out of the Shopping Mall.

The quickest way to the police station was through Old Market Square. They passed the Steamy Café, which faced into the square, and Natty tried not to think of jam doughnuts. Now there was no chance of eating one today, and when they passed the little side street that led to Cosby's Magic Emporium, Jamie glanced wistfully towards his favourite shop.

"Sweet and juicy oranges," cried a stallholder, offering fruit and vegetables. "Bargain offer! Ten for a pound!" Then, quite unexpectedly, the man tossed one, two, three oranges into the air and started juggling. Natty stopped to watch and Jamie did the same, accidentally bumping into a gentleman with a briefcase.

"Watch out!" said the man, side-stepping quickly and hurrying on.

But Jamie lost his balance, slipped on a rotten orange and ended up on his bottom among a pile of cardboard boxes.

Trying not to grin, Natty held out her hand to pull him up. Ignoring the hand because he was cross, Jamie struggled to push himself up, then stopped and, turning on to his knees, began fiddling among the cardboard.

Then, to Natty's surprise, he pulled a grubby handkerchief from his pocket.

"What is it?" she asked.

Holding what he had found carefully with the handkerchief, he lifted up a large brown purse.

"That's Mrs Plumley's," Natty cried, recognizing it at once.

"Don't touch it," said Jamie, standing up. "It might have fingerprints."

"Is there anything left inside?" Natty asked, as the wallet part flapped open.

"There's no money," said Jamie.

"But that plastic card looks like a bus pass."

"What on earth are you two doing?" asked Mum, coming back for them.

Jamie held up the purse. "We've found this in the rubbish!"

"My purse!" cried Mrs Plumley, tottering towards them with all the doubt and dismay of someone realizing there was only one way their purse could have arrived among a pile of rubbish in Old Market Square.

"All the money's gone," said Natty. "Jamie thinks it was the rollerbladers. That they bumped into you on purpose to steal it."

"Oh no," said Mrs Plumley.

"We'll carry on to the police station and report the theft, then take a taxi home," said Mum, gently but firmly in case Mrs Plumley tried to resist. "Our shopping can wait for another day."

But now Mrs Plumley realized she had been robbed, it was as if all the air had gone out of her, and she was left like a deflated balloon. Mum took her bag while Jamie kept hold of the purse.

"What a rotten thing to happen," Mum said, and, agreeing completely, Natty slipped her hand into Mrs Plumley's and held it tight.

Chapter 3
A Brisk Trot to Town

They didn't get home until a lot later and, bursting to tell Ned all about it, Natty ran straight upstairs to her bedroom and closed the door behind her.

"You'll never guess what's happened," she began, stopping at once when she saw the chestnut pony in her special poster had gone. "Ned?" The window was closed; the door was shut. Her eyes lit up with excitement. Ned the magic pony had come to life and was hiding somewhere in her bedroom.

She looked under the chest of drawers and the bed. It wasn't until she turned to the window sill and realized there were four china ponies instead of three that she knew she had found him. "Esmerelda, Prince, Percy and Ned," she counted. Ned was exactly the same size as Percy, the smallest of her china ponies. Natty touched his warm chestnut back with a fingertip.

At once the pony danced into life, no longer pretending to be china. "No," he said, in a ringing tiny voice. "I can't guess what happened." He pranced across the window sill and looked up at her. "Tell me at once." And he pawed the paintwork with a front hoof.

Natty began the story of how the boys on rollerblades had knocked into Mrs Plumley, of the lost purse and how Jamie had found it, of how it still contained Mrs Plumley's pension book and bus pass but not a penny of her money, and how the desk sergeant at the police station had taken down all the details but told them it was unlikely Mrs Plumley would get her money back. Ned snorted his disgust and trotted in a circle.

"But, worst of all," Natty cried, "Mrs Plumley never got round to buying her granddaughter's birthday present! Mum was going to lend her some money, but because Mrs

Plumley was so upset, we only remembered about the present when we got home. I wanted to go back and buy it, but Mum said I couldn't go into town on my own. I've got enough money in my purse for the book. It costs three pounds fifty. I know that from when I read Penelope's copy." Natty slumped on to the window sill and put her chin in her cupped hands. "It's not fair. Now Lucy won't get *Dream Pony* in time for her birthday tea tomorrow."

She stared miserably out of the window. Across the lane, in the field opposite, Penelope Potter's pony

Pebbles was flicking flies in the shade of the hedge. She was about to say that maybe, if she asked her especially nicely, Penelope might give up her copy in exchange for a new one later when she was surprised by an unexpected gust of wind ruffling her hair. Turning round, she found the big Ned squeezed between the bed and the wall, wearing a saddle and bridle.

"Put on your rucksack, open the window and get on," he said. "The plan of action is this. We ride into town and go to the bookshop, where you buy the book. You take it

to Mrs Plumley, who will have it in
time to give to her granddaughter
Lucy tomorrow."

"Ned," cried Natty, "do you think
we can do it?"

"What time do the shops shut?"

"They stay open late at the
Shopping Mall."

"Then what are you waiting for?"

Natty quickly pulled on her
rucksack and flung open the
window.

"And make sure you bring your
purse," said Ned.

"It's in my pocket."

"And we'll keep a look out for

the rollerblading boys. Maybe we can catch those thieves on wheels on the way."

Natty wondered how they would manage such a thing and, still feeling scared of the rollerbladers, thought she would rather leave catching them to the police. But it didn't stop her from jumping on the bed and putting her foot in the stirrup. Mounting from the wrong side was always a little tricky, but she managed it. The moment she was on Ned's back, she found herself dressed in her magic riding clothes, with the usual velvet hard hat, jodhpurs, jodhpur boots and jacket over which, for the first time, was a vivid yellow tabard with black writing on it.

"What does the notice say?" she asked.

"SLOW DOWN FOR HORSES!" replied Ned. "And I hope the drivers will." Natty's rucksack, as usual, had turned into a pair of saddlebags, which were lying behind her across Ned's back. Carrying the book home would be easy. "Ready to go?" the pony asked.

"Yes!" Then, when she realized what Ned was about to do, she cried, "No! Stop!"

She was too late. Ned was already leaning back on his haunches and now he launched himself into the air with a mighty jump. Up they went (it seemed as high as the ceiling!) to leap over the window sill, and Esmerelda, Prince and Percy, into a whirl of magic wind. Natty shut her eyes tight and held fiercely to Ned's mane.

It was only when they landed that she dared open her eyes again. Somehow they had jumped through the open window and were now a tiny pony and rider, balancing on a broad leaf belonging to the fig tree that grew near the wall outside.

"There," said Ned. "You had no problem with that. You've become a very good rider."

"If you say so, Ned," said Natty, who felt herself all of a tremble.

"I do say so," said the pony, and jumped to the leaf below and then the leaf below that, and all the way down the tree to the grass in the front garden, leaving behind a shimmering staircase. The magic wind blew them big again, and with another mighty leap, Ned cleared the garden gate and set off at a brisk trot down the lane.

"Now remember," he said, "you're

wearing the perfect disguise."

"I do remember," said Natty. "I really believe it works."

"Good," said Ned, trotting smartly past Penelope Potter's stable yard.

Penelope looked up from her sweeping as they went by, and Natty instantly forgot the words just spoken.

"I think she recognizes me," she gasped.

"No, she doesn't," whispered Ned. "She recognizes the mystery rider she has seen in the past. Not you."

"My tummy's turning over all the same."

When they reached the junction at the main road, Natty looked back to see Penelope standing in the lane staring after them.

"Never mind Penelope. Keep your mind on the job in hand. Which way do I go? Left or right?"

"Right," said Natty, putting out her right hand to signal. Then, when the road was clear, Ned set off briskly in the direction the bus had taken earlier.

* * *

Natty had no idea until this moment that a pony could extend into such a long, striding trot. It gave a bit of a bumpy ride but covered the ground as fast as a canter, and she soon got used to it. What she couldn't get used to was the traffic. Most cars and lorries slowed down and gave them plenty of space, but the occasional vehicle

came so close that they almost brushed her stirrup iron.

"Not everyone's taking notice of the sign," said Natty.

"No," said Ned. "Just as well I'm not one of those dippy ponies who sees a monster in every crisp bag and shies into the middle of the road."

"It certainly is," said Natty, more glad than she could say.

The trotting pony ate up the miles and they soon left the countryside behind them. The roads became lined with houses and shops, while cars were parked at the kerbsides. As they sped purposefully into the town centre, pedestrians turned to stare.

"We're not going to arrive unnoticed," said Natty. "Everyone's looking at us."

"We're an unusual sight," agreed Ned, trotting under the railway bridge and slowing down. "But not for much longer. Signal left, Natty."

Natty put out her hand and Ned

turned into the narrow road that ran alongside the bridge. Traffic and people were left behind and, apart from one parked car, the street was deserted.

"Quickly," said Ned. "Hop off. It's your turn to carry me."

Natty swung herself to the ground and let go of the reins. There was a swirl of magic wind and Ned vanished along with her riding clothes. Back in her jeans and sweatshirt with her rucksack on her back, she felt less conspicuous but alone until she saw the tiny Ned leaping and bucking at her feet. She pulled off her rucksack and unzipped the front pocket. Ned jumped inside.

"On we go, Natty," he said. "To the Shopping Mall and the bookshop, keeping our eyes peeled for the rollerbladers."

Chapter 4
The Steamy Café

By the time Natty walked into Old Market Square, a few of the stallholders were packing up and she guessed the afternoon was drawing to a close. As her watch had stopped she decided to look through the window at the wall clock in the Steamy Café to find out exactly what time it was.

Peering in, she was startled to see three big boys sitting at the table by the window.

"It's them!" she gasped.

"The rollerbladers?" enquired Ned, popping his nose out from his hiding place in the rucksack. "Where?"

"In the Steamy Café. What shall I do? Run to the police station?"

"There's no time for that. This is just the opportunity we need to find out what they're up to. What can you see?"

"They're talking," said Natty.

"The spiky-haired one's got his rollerblades hanging round his neck, and all three are sitting in their socks."

"What a bit of luck. If we're clever, now that we've found them, we may be able to catch them."

"But Ned, they're big and scary."

"There's no need to worry about that. Just get in there!" And the pony dropped back into his hiding place.

With a shaking hand, Natty pushed open the door and went inside. She glanced towards the rollerbladers but they didn't even

look up. Their heads were together
in deep conversation.

Unsure of what to do, Natty
walked towards the counter. The

only other people in the shop were an old man reading a newspaper and a large lady who was surrounded by shopping bags and chatting to the serving lady.

When Natty appeared at the counter, they stopped. She fished in her pocket for her purse. She would have to buy something.

"Yes?" said the serving lady, looking down at her with raised eyebrows. Sitting in the glass cake displayer was a single jam doughnut. The last of the day.

"A doughnut please," said Natty. The serving lady put the doughnut on a plate and placed it on the counter.

"Anything else?"

"No, thank you."

"Sixty-five pence then, love."

Natty handed over a pound coin and waited for her change. She glanced one more time at the boys.

"We're closing in ten minutes," said the lady, dropping several coins in Natty's hand. "Just so you know."

Natty smiled her thanks and edged her way to the table in the corner under the notice that said:

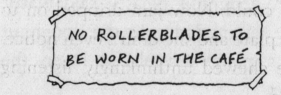

NO ROLLERBLADES TO
BE WORN IN THE CAFÉ

It explained why the boys had taken off their boots. She was about to sit down, leaving her rucksack on for a quick getaway, when she felt a wriggle of protest from inside. Reluctantly, she picked up her doughnut and put it down on the table next to the boys. She pulled up a chair and took a large bite.

Normally Natty would eat a doughnut with care, saving the jammy bit in the middle until last if she could. Now jam dripped on to her plate and she didn't even notice. She chewed unthinkingly, listening hard.

"You're chicken, that's what you are," said the boy with spiky hair in low, urgent tones. "I tell you, it's easy-peasy. We go for another strike now. That's the way to do it. Hit hard and then lay low for a few days."

"Spike, we've got over seventy quid. We don't need to push our luck!"

"We did that in one go, Granger. If we did one more today, we could end up with over a hundred. I say we do it."

One go, Natty realized, probably meant all Mrs Plumley's pension money. At least they hadn't spent it yet.

"Granger's right," said the third boy. "We don't want to push our luck. Seventy pounds is loads."

"For you, maybe," said Spike. "But I intend to live big. I want more."

"Well, I'm with Pete. We've done six hits this week. And we've had it in the Mall, what with no wheels being allowed. The security guard's got our number. Best not overdo it."

"Yeah, but we've only got seventy quid left."

"That's because you keep spending it at the betting shop. It's money down the plughole with you. All gambled away on the horses."

"Keep your voices down," hissed Pete, looking over his shoulder. Natty scooped up a blob of jam with her finger, wishing she was invisible. But it wasn't her that Pete was looking at; it was the women chatting at the counter, and they weren't taking the slightest notice.

"It only needs one horse to win one race and we'll be rich. I've had a tip. Golden Glory! She's racing in the two-thirty at Sandown Park tomorrow. For every pound we put on that horse, we get a hundred back if she wins. That's how good the betting odds are. I'm told she'll win easy."

"Yeah," said Granger. "Who by?"

Spike tapped his nose with a finger. "My secret informant."

"That means the old loser down at the betting shop," groaned Pete.

"Stop moaning. He's a good mate. And if we don't bet a hundred pounds on Golden Glory and she comes in first, we'll be sick," said Spike. Granger looked at Pete questioningly; Pete looked at Granger and shrugged. Spike went on. "I say we nick one more bag, bet what's in it on Golden Glory and win a fortune. What do you say?" He stretched out his hand. "It'll win us ten thousand pounds! But I can't do it on me own."

Granger's face spread with a sly

grin, and he smacked Spike's palm to seal the deal. They waited for Pete. At last, grudgingly, he did the same. When the three boys rose to go, Natty took one last urgent bite of her doughnut and chewed fast, pretending she hadn't been listening. The moment they filed out of the door she was up and after them. They were going to rob someone else, and somehow she and Ned had to stop them. In her haste, she tripped over Spike sitting on the doorstep putting on his rollerblades.

"Watch out," he snarled.

"Sorry," said Natty, hurrying out of the way to take cover behind a pet food stall and peep at them secretly.

"Right," said Ned, whispering

from the rucksack. "We need to set a trap."

"What sort of a trap?" whispered back Natty.

"We need to lure them to a place they can't escape from."

"But how? Once they've got their rollerblades on, I'll never be able to lure them anywhere. Blink and they'll have overtaken me."

"Don't worry," said Ned. "Between us we should manage it."

Natty hoped Ned was right but she had no idea how they would succeed. Fortunately, she didn't have any time to think about it.

The boys were already rollerblading between the market stalls.

"Hurry," said Ned. "What are you waiting for?"

Natty dodged between the shoppers, catching sight of the boys again when they were already halfway across Old Market Square.

"I told you I'd never keep up," she groaned. "They're going to get away."

"No they're not," said Ned. "They'll stop in a minute. You wait. They're looking for a new victim. Someone nice and easy to rob."

An angry crying suddenly filled the square. It came from a little boy who didn't want to get in his pushchair. His mum tried to lift him in, but he wriggled so hard and yelled so loudly that she gave up. Then he refused to walk and sat in the middle of the square, screaming and kicking his legs. People turned to look and the lady grew pink with embarrassment, but the little boy didn't care and carried on making the terrible noise.

The rollerbladers turned back. They came gliding towards the lady, turning, jostling one another and whizzing in circles, all the time spinning closer and closer.

The lady picked up the noisy toddler and in his rage he beat her back with his fists while tears streamed down his pink cheeks. That was until he caught sight of the rollerbladers, at which point his tears stopped and his angry face was transformed by a beaming smile. His

mum turned to where the little boy
pointed, watched the rollerbladers
glide closer and smiled herself.

Granger and Pete began waving
and the little boy waved back.
Both the lady and the little boy
were laughing now. It was then
that Natty saw what the rollerbladers

were after. Hanging over the handle of the pushchair was a handbag. No one seemed to notice Spike slip the bag from the handle and skate off with it.

"Watch out!" shouted Natty. Granger and Pete swung easily away, still waving, following Spike with stylish, lazy footwork. "It's your bag! They've taken your bag!" The lady clearly didn't understand what she was shouting about. This left Natty no choice. She didn't wait for the loss to be discovered. She raced after the rollerbladers as fast as she could.

Chapter 5
The Chase

Natty dodged between the startled shoppers and pelted from Old Market Square. She caught a glimpse of the boys disappearing from the High Street into a side road. She knew the way they had taken led to a puzzle of little back streets, and the boys would be quickly lost if she didn't hurry. She ran her fastest, hoping that Ned wasn't being too jostled in the rucksack, but there was nothing she could do about it. She turned off the High Street and stopped. There was a delivery van parked, but other than that, the street was empty.

"They've gone!"

"Don't give up," said Ned, peeping from the rucksack pocket. "They can't be far away." Spurred on, Natty ran past the van to a tiny crossroads. Then she saw them, off to the right, three looping, twirling boys, tossing the bag to one another in a victory game of catch.

"Quick," said Ned, "grab the bag before they stop to look inside."

Natty wasn't quite sure how to do this. She retreated behind the van, heart pounding, as the boys, cocky with their success, looped and spun towards her.

"What we need," said Ned, "is a nice dead-end alleyway."

"I know of one," said Natty. "It leads to the timber yard on the other side of the square. Dad goes there for his wood. It's got big black gates."

"Remember what I said about luring them into a trap," said Ned. "Well, the stolen bag's the bait; the timber yard the trap."

"Yes, if we could get them inside, we could lock them in. I'm sure the timber-yard man would help."

The boys were drawing level, and Natty crouched low, ready to spring, keeping her eyes glued to the flying handbag. It went from Spike to Granger to Pete, then back towards Spike. Only it didn't reach him. With an outstretched hand, Natty leapt her highest and caught it.

All three boys stopped and, in the moment of surprise that followed, Natty turned and fled into a delivery area at the back of a shop, clutching her prize. Arriving at an open door and grateful for such luck, she plunged through it to find herself in a storeroom full of boxes, boots and trainers, and was quick to realize she had come in the rear entrance of a shoe shop.

She had no time to lose if she was going to beat the boys to the timber yard. Already she could hear Spike shouting to the others to go round to the High Street and cut her off. She raced forwards, jumping the clutter on the floor, and pushed her way through the door ahead to the shop, startling an assistant on her way to the storeroom. The pile of boxes the girl was carrying went flying.

"Sorry," cried Natty, pushing past.

Keeping a tight hold of the stolen handbag, she raced for the front door and burst on to the pavement. There was no sign yet of her pursuers and she ran her hardest back towards Old Market Square. As she turned into the square she looked back, and her gaze drew the rollerbladers to her. Now they had seen her and it gave her only seconds to reach the alleyway on the other side of the square. Not time enough.

Clutching the handbag to her, she did the only thing she could think of. She dived under the nearest stall and started crawling. Beyond the pretend grass cover that draped the stall's sides, she heard the whirr of rollerblade wheels spinning past.

"Come out, little girl. We know you're there. We're gonna find you and then you'll be sorry."

It was Spike, and his words made her heart race. How he and the others dared come back to the square was a source of amazement to her. But dare they did, and so far nobody seemed to be after them. She wondered what had happened to the lady and the little boy. But she didn't wonder for long. She had to make sure the coast was clear before dodging underneath another stall where she found herself clambering between potato sacks.

"Keep going, you're doing really well," said Ned encouragingly in her ear. Natty sprang across the walkway and ducked behind a sweet stall.

"Hey, you," cried the stallholder. "Clear off! Don't think you're nicking my sweets." Bursting out on the other side, Natty caught sight of the grim-faced sweet-seller and raced for cover further away under a fabric stall. Here she had plenty of space for a breather, and fortunately was noticed by nobody.

Now there was only one more row of stalls before the alleyway that led to Newbury and Sons, the timber yard. The yard's impressive black iron gates had always been open when she had been there with Dad, but Natty imagined that when shut at night, they were excellent at keeping out burglars. And what would keep out burglars would also keep in rollerbladers. But, best of all, she was sure the cheery timber-yard man would help her capture the boys.

She eyed the distance to the alleyway. It would take a few seconds of fast sprinting to get there. She crouched low, waiting for the right moment. The rollerbladers rounded the end stall and came towards her.

"Ned, hold tight! I'm going to go now!" She shot from under the stall, did a couple of on-the-spot leaps until she was certain the boys had seen her, then bolted out of the square down the alleyway. Panting hard, she raced between the strong black gates into the yard. The place was deserted – no Newbury & Sons lorry, no cheery timber-yard man.

Of all the luck, he was out on a
delivery, and piles of planks and the
smell of sawdust were not going to
be enough to shelter her. Now what
was she to do?

A sudden breeze lifted the hair on
the back of her head. "Get on!" said
the familiar voice of the big Ned.

He stood, tacked up and ready, behind her. With all the haste she could muster, Natty flung herself into the saddle. At once the magic wind blew, leaving a minuscule Ned to gallop away with a tiny Natty clasping an even tinier stolen handbag. By the time the boys spun into the yard, pony and rider were hidden beneath a plank.

"I can hear a police siren," cried Pete. "We've got to clear out of here."

"Not before we get the bag back from that girl. She's in here somewhere," said Spike, his voice full of menace. "Once I get my hands on her, she's going to pay for this."

Sawdust swirled about their hiding place and Natty found herself staring straight at the wheels of Spike's rollerblades. The dust seeped into her throat and she stifled a cough. Thank goodness he didn't think to look under the plank near his feet.

"Leave it. It's only betting money," said Granger. "If we don't watch it, we'll get caught."

"Not if you stick with me," said Spike. "I'm lucky."

"A-a-atishoo!" Natty pinched her nose but too late.

"Give us that bit of wood, Pete. There's something under here."

Ned backed further into the dark as two giant eyes peered under the plank. The eyes blinked and a hand jabbed a piece of wood the size of a tree trunk into their hiding place – once, then twice. Natty ducked and clung on to Ned's neck.

"What you wasting time for?" said Granger.

"I heard something."

"There's only room for mice under them planks, daft head."

The boys moved further into the yard and, seizing his moment, Ned set off at a gallop for the entrance. Covering this wide open space seemed to take for ever, and Natty glanced over her shoulder, terrified the boys would come back and mow them down. But once the great gates loomed above them, the magic wind blew them big again.

"Quickly," ordered Ned. "Pull the gates closed."

Natty leaned forward and grabbed the nearest gate, while Ned backed round until it clanged shut. The noise brought the boys racing from the back of the yard.

"What the blooming hell do you think you're doing?" yelled Spike.

Natty pulled at the other gate. It seemed to swing in slow motion, and for one dreadful moment she thought the boys were going to escape. But it clanged shut at last just as the rollerbladers reached it. They banged and thumped and yelled, but they couldn't get out – not with Ned leaning his rump against the gates to keep them closed.

Ned took the stolen bag in his teeth while Natty quickly wrapped the waiting chain between the two handles and locked the gates

together. Then, finally, Ned hung
the handbag over a handle.

"Open the gates! Open them! I'll
get you for this! I'll get you!" yelled
Spike in a fury.

"Now what?" asked Natty, panting hard after all her effort.

"We'll go and buy Mrs Plumley's book," said Ned, as if it were that simple.

The police siren grew louder by the second.

"But how will the police know where to find the thieves?"

Outraged banging set the chain rattling. There were more yells.

"You can tell them," said Ned. "Besides, with all that noise the boys are giving themselves away."

Then, before Natty had a chance to dismount, the lady with the

pushchair wheeled the little boy
into the alleyway, and following her
came the first of several policemen.

"Now's your chance," whispered
the pony, trotting to meet them,
while behind them the black gates
swayed.

"The thieves are locked in the timber yard," explained Natty to the surprised lady and the even more surprised policemen, none of whom expected to find a little girl on a prancing chestnut pony blocking their way. "I locked them in."

"Horsey!" cried the small boy in the pushchair gleefully.

"And your stolen bag is hanging on the gate!" Natty told the lady. Arching his neck, Ned frolicked sideways. "I'd better go. My pony's getting restless," said the mystery rider.

More onlookers arrived, and at
the sight of the frisking pony, the
crowd parted, allowing Ned to trot
out of the alleyway and between
the stalls of Old Market Square.
He nipped behind a trader's lorry
and, when he was sure no one was

looking, the magic wind blew them tiny again, and a miniature pony and rider trotted to safety underneath a stall so that Natty could get off.

"That's a good job done," said Ned as he jumped into the rucksack pocket. "Now which way to the bookshop?"

"It's this way," said Natty and, emerging without being noticed, they set off towards the Shopping Mall as fast as they could.

Chapter 6
"Dream Pony"

In the Mall Natty jumped from the top of the escalator just at the moment when the cascading fountain changed from pink to yellow. She hardly noticed because she was looking straight ahead to Worrels Bookshop. She had never been in a bookshop on her own before – not that she was alone with Ned in her rucksack pocket, but it did feel strange. She walked in through the door wondering where the children's section would be. The assistant at the till looked at Natty over her spectacles in such a fierce way that Natty almost turned round and went out again.

"I'm looking for the children's books," she said, plucking up her courage.

The assistant pointed. "They're at the back of the shop."

What Natty found was an unexpectedly friendly nook, with

cushions on the floor and a large teddy bear. With her rucksack slung over one shoulder, she could see Ned's tiny head looking along the shelves.

"What was the book called again?" he asked.

"*Dream Pony*," said Natty. She leaned her rucksack against a cushion and ran a finger across the row of book spines. "I wish I could remember who wrote it. They put books in alphabetical order, don't they?"

"Yes, they do!"

The voice made her jump. The

assistant had followed her down the shop and was once again regarding Natty over her spectacles. Natty glanced down at the rucksack and felt foolish. After all, the lady must have thought she was talking to herself. Fortunately, there was no sign of Ned.

"Which book are you looking for?"

"*Dream Pony*," said Natty shyly.

"Ah yes, by Ginny Green." The lady looked along the middle shelf. "No, I'm sorry, we seem to have sold the last copy."

Natty, who so badly wanted to surprise Mrs Plumley with it, felt her heart sink. "Oh!" she said. "Oh dear!"

"I can order it for you if you like."

"No ... no, thank you. I wanted it for today."

"I'm sorry. But there are other pony books. There might be one that takes your fancy. I'll leave you to browse, shall I?" The assistant padded back to

the front of the shop, and Natty
wondered if she was right – maybe
another pony book would do.

She looked aimlessly along the
rows, thinking how difficult it was to
choose, when there was a rush of
magic wind. She turned round to
find the big Ned filling the children's
books section, nosing along the top
shelf. With a swish of his tail he
gently wobbled his lips around the
spine of a book and took it in his
teeth. Turning to the surprised Natty,
he dropped it into her open palms.

"Someone put it back in the wrong
place," he said. "Lucky I spotted it."

Natty recognized the cover at once. "This is it!" she exclaimed, and then glanced anxiously over her shoulder. She didn't want to be thrown out of the bookshop for bringing in a pony. "You found it. Thank you." And she gave Ned a big hug. Then suddenly he was gone again and her arms were shaped around thin air.

"Did you call?" the assistant asked.

"No, but look!" Natty held up the copy of *Dream Pony* triumphantly. "You did have it after all!"

"Oh good," said the assistant. "I must have missed it!" She smiled, and

Natty saw she wasn't so fierce after all. She gave the assistant the book and quickly checked Ned was back in the rucksack. Now all she had to do was pay and they could go home.

Arriving back in the little side road by the railway bridge, Ned sprang from the rucksack pocket and in no time he was his big self, ready for Natty to mount. Once she was on his back, smart in her magic riding clothes, and had checked that *Dream Pony* was safely stowed in a saddlebag, she was ready to go. Ned turned back to the main road.

"What do you say about us returning home across country?" he asked. "I think I can find our way back that way. It's rush hour and no fun on a busy road."

"Yes, please," cried Natty, eyes alight. It would be just like her earlier pretend on the bus, only this time it would be real.

"Then as soon as we get out of town, that's what we'll do," said Ned, and set off with the same ground-covering trot that he had used to get them there.

It wasn't long before fields spread out on either side of the road and, with an energetic bound, Ned soared over a gate and set off at a steady canter, making the wind whistle in Natty's ears. She loved leaping hedges and ditches.

It was better than anything and she crouched in the stirrups with a big grin on her face.

When they finally landed in Pebbles's field, they kept out of sight behind the hedge while Natty swung herself from the saddle. The moment she let go of the reins, the big Ned was gone, leaving Natty to watch the tiny Ned trot under the gate. Her window was still open, and as she climbed from the field she could see the fig leaves tremble as a tiny pony sprang from leaf to leaf all the way back to her bedroom.

But before Natty could go indoors

she had an important delivery to make. She opened Mrs Plumley's front gate and went up to the door. She knocked once and heard Ruddles bark a warning to his owner. While waiting she took the book from her rucksack and clutched it to her. At last Mrs Plumley opened the door, and Ruddles wagged his tail.

"Hello, boy," she said, giving him a pat. "Hello, Mrs Plumley. Are you feeling better?"

"A lot better, thank you, Natty dear," replied her friend. "Are you going to come in?"

"I'd better not," said Natty,

remembering that no one knew she had gone out and that by now she might have been missed. "But I've got you this for Lucy's birthday."

Mrs Plumley took the offered package and looked inside. "Goodness me," she said, smiling. "Wherever did you get it?"

Natty thought fast. She didn't want to tell a lie but couldn't tell the truth, or at least not all of it. "A friend found it for me," she said. "In a bookshop. It's the one you wanted."

"Natty, you're a little darling!" said Mrs Plumley, and planted a big

kiss on her cheek.
"Thank you. It
makes up for my
terrible day."

"Not quite
so terrible any
more," said
Natty. "I think the
rollerbladers have been caught so
you should get your money back."

"Oh, I do hope so," said Mrs
Plumley, the usual twinkle lighting
up her eyes. "Thank you for the book,
Natty dear. I shall wrap it up ready
and pay you back as soon as I can."

After she had said goodbye to

Mrs Plumley, Natty raced to her house and in through the back door.

"And where have you been?" Mum asked, busy in the kitchen. "I thought you were upstairs."

"Not far," said Natty.

"Miaow!" Tabitha wound herself around Natty's legs to say hello, and was quickly picked up.

"Hello, beautiful cat, have you missed me?" Tabitha had, and to show how much, she purred loudly and leaned her front paws over Natty's shoulder, digging in her claws. Used to these pinpricks, Natty hugged her. She was interrupted by

a mighty cheer from the living
room, which sent her running.

"They've caught the rollerbladers,"
shouted Jamie. "It's on the news.
Look!"

And there it was, a report on
the television. A stallholder from Old
Market Square was telling how a
mystery rider had locked the thieves

in Newbury and Sons, the timber yard, and then had surprisingly disappeared.

"Cool!" said Jamie. "I bet you wish the mystery rider was you."

"I might," said Natty, nuzzling her nose into Tabitha's fur to hide an unstoppable grin. Then, clutching her furry bundle, she hurried upstairs to tell Ned.

The End